Disney

Before the Story

Pocahontas

LEADS THE WAY

By

TESSA ROEHL

ILLUSTRATED BY

ROSA LA BARBERA

DISNEP PRESS

Los Angeles • New York

For Jill, Ryan, and Lady Unicorn
—T.R.

Special thank-you to Dawn Jackson
(Saginaw Chippewa), Cultural Consultant

FAC-029261-20234

Library of Congress Control Number: 2019957719

ISBN 978-1-368-06260-2

Printed in the United States of America

First Paperback Edition, September 2020

10 9 8 7 6 5 4 3 2 1

Lexile: 710L

Book design by Margie Peng

Visit disneybooks.com

SUSTAINABLE
FORESTRY
INITIATIVE

Certified Sourcing

www.sfiprogram.org
SFI-01415

Chapter 1
Summer Harvest

The summer sun shone hot on Pocahontas's shoulders. It made her feel restored, like a bud reaching the earth's surface and drinking in the rays of energy to make it grow—just as the bean crop around her had done, coming to life bold and plentiful in the sun.

She plucked a bean and dropped it in her basket. She smiled to herself, thinking what a marvel it was that every year these crops that fed and nourished her village were planted alongside the corn and the squash, each working to help the others grow: The cornstalks provided the bean vines something to hold on to and grow tall, while the beans helped breathe life into the corn. The squash leaves below shaded and protected both the corn and the beans. It was a kind of magic, and Pocahontas never grew tired of discovering new ways this magic showed itself in the land.

"No!" A little boy's shout tore Pocahontas away from her thoughts.

Pocahontas glanced toward the sound. Nakoma, a girl close to Pocahontas's age, was picking beans, too. Tomoy, Nakoma's little brother, had been a handful all day, tugging on Nakoma's skirt, complaining about the heat, and refusing to follow any of Nakoma's instructions.

Nakoma was trying to get Tomoy to help her fill her basket, but Tomoy wasn't helping at all. He was just hiding in the plants for shade. On the other side of Nakoma's ankles, her younger sister, Alawa, was dutifully picking the beans just the way Nakoma was showing her.

Nakoma caught Pocahontas watching them. "You're doing it wrong, you know," Nakoma called over.

Pocahontas paused, clutching the beans

she had just picked. She looked at her hands, confused.

"You should pick them top to bottom, in rows. The way you're doing it, one at a time, from all different places on the vines—you're going to miss some," Nakoma said.

Pocahontas forced herself to smile. "I'll keep that in mind."

She returned her attention to the bean plants. *That's why we aren't friends,* Pocahontas thought. Even though Nakoma had enough of her own chores to focus on, she still found time to tell everyone else what they should be doing and how they should be doing it. And she *always* had to follow the rules.

Sometimes when Pocahontas watched Nakoma with her siblings, she'd feel a pang of jealousy, wishing she had such close companions. And she'd wonder if she should try a little harder and give the other girl a chance. Maybe they'd become friends after all.

But then Nakoma would say or do something that reminded Pocahontas just how different they were. So Pocahontas would give up any hope that the two might become close.

Pocahontas sighed and looked down at the river below, beyond the gardens and lodges. The water was much higher than usual for the summer. It had rained nonstop for the past three days, which had worried the village, as they were losing precious time to harvest their crops. Nakoma was right about one thing: efficiency was more important than ever. There was extra pressure to get all the beans, corn, and squash picked and stored so the tribe would have food to last through winter.

Pocahontas never minded the work. But sometimes, when she was doing the same thing over and over and *over* again, it was hard not to get distracted. That rushing river water was so irresistible. Pocahontas closed her eyes, feeling the sun on her shoulders, letting the other sounds fade away until all she could

hear was the river in the distance—water tumbling, journeying, rushing off somewhere new; always, always *going*.

Then cries broke through Pocahontas's moment of peace. Tomoy was wailing at his sister's feet. Nakoma tried to shush him, with little effect.

Pocahontas set down her basket of beans and walked over to them. "Hey there, little one." She crouched next to the boy. "What's the matter?"

Nakoma folded her arms. "He always does this," she said. "Whenever there's work to be done, he whines and complains and finds excuses." She huffed. "This time he says he doesn't feel well."

"I'm hot," the boy sobbed.

"It's summer, Tomoy. Of course it's hot. This is the first time we've seen sun in three days," Nakoma said.

"Sometimes just looking at the river can help cool me down," Pocahontas said. "I like to imagine wading in and letting the water rush around my ankles. We can do that after we're done picking the crops. What do you say?"

Tomoy sniffled, still crying. "I want to go *now*!"

Pocahontas looked at the little boy. His thick, dark hair was clinging to his forehead, damp with sweat.

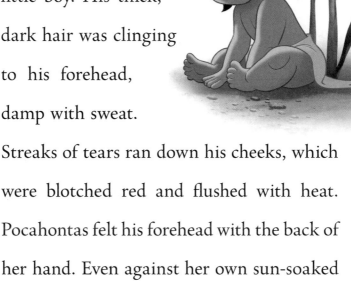

Streaks of tears ran down his cheeks, which were blotched red and flushed with heat. Pocahontas felt his forehead with the back of her hand. Even against her own sun-soaked skin, Tomoy's face felt like it was on fire.

"I think he has a fever," Pocahontas said to Nakoma.

Nakoma kneeled down, looking stunned. "What?" She felt her brother's forehead.

"Oh, no—I thought—I just assumed he was trying to get attention."

She turned to her younger sister. "Alawa," Nakoma said, her face full of worry. "Go fetch Mother, now!"

The little girl ran to find their mother among the other village women picking beans. Nakoma lifted Tomoy into her arms, and he cried even harder. "I'm sorry," Nakoma said, her voice soft. "I'm sorry I didn't listen."

Nakoma looked down at her basket, only half full of beans.

"Don't worry," Pocahontas said. "I'll finish this section."

Nakoma nodded and rushed off in the direction Alawa had run. Pocahontas watched them go. She'd never felt such a terrible fever. She wondered if Tomoy would be all right. Glancing back at the river, Pocahontas closed her eyes once more, focusing all her energy in that direction.

Send some of your cool relief to Tomoy, Pocahontas thought, willing the river to listen. *He needs it.*

Chapter 2
The Healer

Pocahontas filled up her basket and Nakoma's as quickly as she could before she ran down to the healer in the village. Word had already spread about Tomoy's fever, and other people were beginning to gather as well. Everyone wanted to know what they could do to help the boy.

Pocahontas joined the group standing outside, trying to peek over their shoulders and around their waists to see what was happening. Pocahontas could just make out the shape of her father, Powhatan, the chief of her people. His large, commanding presence was easy enough to spot from far away. But that was all she could see.

Nakoma was standing off to the side of the small crowd, clutching her little sister's hand. She looked miserable.

"Does Kekata know what's wrong?" Pocahontas asked Nakoma.

"He's examining Tomoy and helping to keep him cool. We're supposed to stay away in case he's contagious." Nakoma sniffled.

Pocahontas put her hand on Nakoma's

shoulder and waited with her. Finally, the healer, Kekata, emerged from the lodge with Chief Powhatan and Nakoma's parents.

"Tomoy has a high fever," Kekata said, addressing the crowd. The whole village tended to be involved when a tribe member fell ill, both to help out as needed and to be cautious in case the sickness spread. "I've seen this kind of illness before, though not often. I have enough medicine to get him through the next couple of nights. But he's very ill. I will need to make more of this medicine — otherwise the boy will not survive."

Next to Pocahontas, Nakoma let out a small whimper.

"What do you require to make the medicine, Kekata?" Pocahontas's father asked. "We'll send a team to fetch whatever it is."

"The ingredient I need is an herb, a white flowering plant that blooms in the shape of soft fingers. I was going to make a trip to replenish my supply a few days ago, but then the rains came." Kekata held up a dried plant. Tiny white buds dotted the green stem, giving it the appearance of a thick tail feather. "This is the last one I have, which I'll use in Tomoy's medicine tonight. It grows plentifully in a grove to the north. It will take about two days in either direction."

"Then we'll send our fastest men," Chief Powhatan said. "Mingan, Pikwa, Wahun — you'll set out immediately and bring back as much as you can carry." The three strong village men nodded in agreement.

Pocahontas stared at the plant Kekata was holding. Like the rest of the tribe, she'd been taught from a young age to identify all the plants that grew around her: what was safe for eating, good for medicine, practical for shelter, and helpful for other uses. She didn't know the name of this plant, but she was sure she'd seen it before.

Pocahontas spoke up. "Wait!" Her father, Kekata, Nakoma, and the rest of the crowd turned to look at the daughter of the chief. "I saw this plant down the river. It's just off the bank." She looked at Chief Powhatan. "Father, when we were fishing last month, I went ashore and gathered raspberries, remember? I'm sure I saw this plant growing next to the berry patch."

"Pocahontas," her father began, using the voice he always did when he was going to tell his daughter no.

She continued quickly before he could go on. "I'm sure it was there. It looked just like that plant."

Kekata nodded thoughtfully. "It may be that you saw the plant there, Pocahontas. But with the heavy rains of the last few days, the river is swollen and flooded. The waters are too rough for the men to journey safely downriver. The rapids will be almost impassable."

"But it will be much faster than the trip you described," Pocahontas protested. "It might only take one day instead of the four days it will take to get to the grove to the north and back!"

"Pocahontas," the chief said firmly, "if our men get caught in the rapids and drown, then not only will Tomoy not have the medicine he needs, but we'll have lost more of our people. Everyone would be worse off than before." He nodded to the men chosen to make the journey. "We'll proceed with the plan to go north."

With the chief's words, the crowd of villagers broke up and everyone began to return to their usual activities.

Pocahontas was disappointed. She knew how high the water was; she'd been watching it rush and churn and tumble all day. But weren't her people supposed to be brave? Wasn't the health of little Tomoy worth the risk?

"Go on," she heard Nakoma say. Alawa

had been tugging at her arm, begging to run to her mother. Nakoma let the little one go, and Nakoma's mother scooped Alawa into her arms, kissing the hair on her youngest child's head.

Pocahontas watched the men pack their blankets and supplies, getting ready for the foraging trip. She watched her father speak with Kekata and Nakoma's parents in a hushed voice. She watched the other villagers store the day's crops, care for the young children, begin the evening's dinners, and set about all the other usual tasks for that time of day.

And then she watched Nakoma, whose

face was filled with deep sadness for her brother. Pocahontas knew that look of grief. She'd seen it on her own father's face on the rare occasion someone mentioned her mother. But unlike with her mother, who had passed away years before when Pocahontas was a baby, this time Pocahontas could do something.

"Come with me," Pocahontas said to Nakoma. "I have an idea."

Pocahontas ushered Nakoma away from Kekata's lodge and the activity of the village. She led her closer to the river, where the rushing water would drown out any chance of their being overheard.

"What's going on?" Nakoma asked.

"I'm *sure* I saw that plant your brother needs for his medicine. And if I'm right, we can pick it and get back long before the warriors return. Even before Tomoy needs his next dose. It will give him a much better chance to survive," Pocahontas said.

"*We* can pick it?" Nakoma raised her eyebrows. "How would we do that?"

"We'll take a canoe," Pocahontas said.

"But you heard your father and Kekata. The waters are too dangerous."

"I've gone down the river fishing with my father a million times," Pocahontas said. "I'm sure I've been on the river when it was this high before. And anyway, we really wouldn't be going that far."

Nakoma looked at the river. Pocahontas wondered if Nakoma heard what she did: the water almost begging the girls to jump in, its current running and pointing in the direction of the plant that would heal Nakoma's brother.

"It's been calling me all day," Pocahontas said softly. "My father has shown me all the tricks for avoiding the most dangerous parts."

"While you were listening to the river, I should have been listening to Tomoy," Nakoma said. "Then maybe we would have realized he was sick sooner—and people would already be on their way to bring the cure." She wiped a tear falling down her cheek. "I owe this to him." She turned to Pocahontas, her eyes determined. "Let's go."

Chapter 3
A Journey Begins

Taking care to remain unseen, Pocahontas and Nakoma walked along the river to the place where the tribe's dugout canoes were stored. The boats were all made from tree trunks that had been burned in patches, then scraped and smoothed out to form a hollow, round-bottomed space inside. Some canoes were so large they could hold up to forty men. Pocahontas knew that would be more than she and Nakoma could handle.

"That one should do." Pocahontas pointed at one of the smaller canoes, which fortunately was at the edge of the collection of boats. Several paddles rested inside. Nakoma and Pocahontas began to push and drag the boat toward the river. The ground was coated with slime and mud from the river water, which helped the canoe glide along in spite of its weight.

When they reached the riverbank, the girls stopped and watched the water. Pocahontas could see that it did actually look higher and choppier than she'd noticed before. There was usually a drop down to the water, but now it sloshed up and over the sides of the bank.

"You're sure you can navigate this?" Nakoma asked, staring at the water.

Pocahontas looked behind them at the village. No one had noticed the girls moving the canoe. No one was going to stop them.

"I can do it. We can do it. We've been on this river and in these boats our whole lives," Pocahontas said. "On the count of three?"

Nakoma nodded.

The girls pushed the canoe up to the water's edge. They gripped the wood tight

as the water lapped around the nose of the boat, trying to grab it and pull it along in the current.

"One . . . two . . ." the girls counted together, bending their knees in a crouch so they could spring forward quickly, "three!"

On *three*, Nakoma and Pocahontas shoved the boat in the water and jumped in. The canoe immediately lurched away from the bank. Pocahontas quickly grabbed one of the paddles and shoved it against a river rock to help straighten out the boat. The canoe shot down the river, the sound of rushing water filling Pocahontas's ears with its song. She breathed in the crisp, clean air and skimmed her fingers along the frothing surface. This was her favorite place to be: on the water, in a boat, on her way *somewhere*.

"And away we go!" Pocahontas cheered, twisting around to see Nakoma behind her.

Nakoma was wearing a very different expression. Her face was almost as gray as the rocks near the bank. "Are you sure we aren't going too fast?" she asked in a small voice.

"No such thing!" Pocahontas shouted, grinning. She tipped her head back and watched the towering evergreen trees rush past. She imagined the branches pushing their canoe along, helping the girls move swiftly. Birds perched overhead, the only creatures who might have felt freer than Pocahontas did. On the shore, a deer, munching on some plants, looked up as the canoe bobbed past. Pocahontas waved.

"Pocahontas!" Nakoma cried.

Nakoma was pointing shakily downriver. Pocahontas followed her gaze and looked at the waters ahead. The rapids were approaching—fast.

This was the part of the river that had worried Chief Powhatan and Kekata and made them decide the trip was too dangerous. The rapids had come up much sooner than Pocahontas had expected, likely because the whole river was moving faster than normal.

The rapids were always dangerous, but they were a part of the daily life of the Powhatan people when they went down-river. On the calmest days, the rapids would gently dip the canoes in a few spots. On the most treacherous days, it required a good amount of paddling to keep the boats on a steady course. But Pocahontas had gone through these rapids so many times with her father she had the motions memorized.

"Grab a paddle!" Pocahontas shouted to Nakoma.

"I've got one!" Nakoma shouted back.

As their canoe approached the rapids, the sound of the river grew louder and louder, crashing against rocks, tumbling and hurrying to get wherever it needed to go.

The first rapid loomed ahead. Pocahontas knew from her father to look for what he called the tongues of the rapids: the center, where all the water was pushing. This would help guide the boat through the rapid naturally.

"Do you see that shape that's forming

in the water over there, like a triangle?" Pocahontas yelled.

"Yes!" Nakoma yelled back.

"Paddle toward it—now!" The girls threw all their weight into paddling hard toward the spot in the rapid.

As the canoe got closer to the rapid, river spray blasted the girls, coming from every direction. Pocahontas kept paddling hard. She knew Nakoma was keeping up with her because the boat was staying on its path. The rapid gushed its water down the river in a wave, creating a small but steep drop on the other side. The canoe hit the rapid, causing their boat to sail through the air for a moment before it landed safely.

"Now paddle left!" Pocahontas yelled over her shoulder. The next rapid was coming up fast, and they'd have to navigate around the rock in their path quickly.

"*What?*" Nakoma shouted back. It was hard to hear her over the roiling rapids.

"Left!" Pocahontas shouted. "Paddle left!"

The girls paddled and paddled as hard as they could, though against the force of the current, it felt like they were tiny minnows trying to swim upstream. Still, the boat shifted in the direction Pocahontas knew it needed to go. They narrowly avoided the large rock in the center of the river before the canoe crashed over the next rapid.

Phew! Pocahontas sighed in relief. And then, just as she was about to shout to Nakoma to paddle right, she saw another rock directly in their path. A rock that had never been there before. A rock that must have been swept up in the flash flooding over the past few days and was completely blocking their path. There was nowhere to go, no time to go anywhere but directly into it.

CRUNCH.

Chapter 4
A Rocky Start

"Ahhh!" Nakoma screamed. The canoe was shoved up against the rock, stuck in place by the force of the river.

"Help me push!" Pocahontas cried. She used her paddle against the rock, trying to shove the canoe loose. Nakoma did the same. The girls pushed and pushed, river water splashing over their arms and hands, making their grips slippery. Eventually, they got the boat away from the rock. As soon as it was free, the canoe ripped down the river and hurtled toward the next rapid.

"What do we do?" Nakoma yelled.

Pocahontas's arms ached. The rapids had never been anywhere close to this intense. She knew she'd completely underestimated the power of a few days of rain. But they had to keep going.

"Paddle right!" Pocahontas pointed to the opening in between a few rocks. The girls headed toward it, making slow progress against the current. They just made it to the gap, scraping against the rocks on the left side as the canoe slipped through.

Then, before Pocahontas could prepare
for it, the next rapid was upon them. "Hold
on!" Pocahontas shouted. Nakoma screamed
as the boat went over the rapid at an angle. It
crashed into the water, which spun the boat
around like a twig. Suddenly, the girls were
moving down the river backward.

"Oh, no!" Nakoma shouted.

"Turn around," Pocahontas yelled. The girls switched directions in their seats. Nakoma was now sitting in front and facing downriver.

"I lost hold of my paddle!" Nakoma cried. Pocahontas went to grab another one from the floor of the canoe. She gulped. There was only one left. The others had been thrown overboard in the chaos of the rapid. She handed Nakoma the last paddle and hoped the worst was behind them.

But it wasn't. Even though Pocahontas knew how to navigate the rapids, the current was simply too strong. The canoe hit rock after rock, its wooden frame making terrifying crunching sounds. The girls had to use every bit of their strength to steer through the obstacles.

Finally, the rapids eased and the canoe was back on level water. Pocahontas pulled her paddle up and dropped it on the floor of the canoe. She rubbed her sore arms.

"That's it, right?" Nakoma asked, trying to catch her breath. "We made it through?"

Pocahontas nodded. "We made it."

Nakoma pulled her paddle out of the water but stopped before she dropped it in the bottom of the canoe. "Um, Pocahontas. Look."

Pocahontas followed Nakoma's gaze.

The paddle Pocahontas had dropped inside the canoe was floating on almost an inch of water. Both girls were drenched from the rapids, so Pocahontas hadn't noticed the water creeping over her feet.

"Maybe it's from the rapids spraying us with water?" Pocahontas tried to ignore the memory of the sound of splintering wood as they crashed up against the rocks. "Let's try getting some of this out."

The girls cupped their hands and began to scoop water out of the boat and back into the river. The tiny handfuls felt useless, but they worked as fast as they could, their arms screaming for rest.

"It's not working," Nakoma panted. "The water is getting higher." She stood up and walked down the length of the canoe, her feet sloshing in the water. She kneeled, running her finger on the side near the bottom. "There's water getting in here." She kept searching. "And here, and here, and—ahh!" She stood back as one of the cracks splintered and more water gushed in.

"We have to get to shore—right now!" Pocahontas said. She grabbed her paddle and tossed Nakoma the other. "Over there."

The girls paddled the canoe to land, near a clearing visible on the bank ahead. They used the last bit of strength in their muscles to pull the canoe up onto the shore, then collapsed next to it.

They were both soaked to their bones, their bodies exhausted from the effort of navigating through the rapids. Then, with the sun shining down, promising warmth, dry clothes, and a chance to rest, both girls curled up and fell asleep within moments.

Chapter 5
Facing Facts

When Pocahontas opened her eyes, it took her a minute to remember where she was and why. She was outside, on the ground in an unfamiliar place. Not on her sleeping mat at home, where she would be snuggled under deerskins, warm and safe in the smoky air from the fire that was always going in the middle of the room.

Instead she was on a riverbank. Her

clothes and hair were dry but stiff. The sun was hanging low in the sky. Pocahontas knew it would be gone within the hour.

"Nakoma, wake up." She shook the other girl awake. Nakoma murmured and rubbed her eyes. She blinked a few times, then shot upright.

"I was hoping it was just a terrible nightmare," Nakoma groaned.

"I'm afraid not," Pocahontas said.

Nakoma stood, brushing off her clothes. "I can't believe this. What are we going to do? We have to get home."

"I don't think that's going to happen tonight," Pocahontas said.

"Why not?" Nakoma asked.

"Well . . ." Pocahontas scratched her head. Wasn't it obvious? "The boat is full of holes. It needs to be repaired."

"So we'll walk back," Nakoma said.

"I don't think that's safe," Pocahontas said. "It will be dark soon."

"Not safe?" Nakoma sneered. "Taking the canoe out wasn't safe, either, but we did that."

Pocahontas knew Nakoma was upset. She didn't blame her. But she also knew that it wouldn't do any good to get hurt or lost walking through the woods in the dark. "We're better off staying here for the night, building a fire, and figuring out a plan in the morning."

Nakoma folded her arms. She looked so angry Pocahontas was afraid she might explode. "I thought you said you knew how to get around those rapids!" Nakoma yelled. "I never should have listened to you."

Pocahontas felt ashamed. "I *do* know how to get around them, but . . . I guess I didn't realize how much the rain would affect the river. It was foolish of me."

"We won't make it home tonight, and my parents will have no idea why," Nakoma said. "They're already worried about my brother. Now I've made it worse,

because they'll be worried about me, too."

Pocahontas felt awful. Her father would be worrying just as much as Nakoma's parents. "I'm sorry. I really am. I just wanted to help."

Nakoma shook her head and walked to the canoe. She craned her neck over the edge, searching the bottom of the boat.

"What are you looking for?" Pocahontas asked.

"Mats for shelter," Nakoma answered. "We'd better get to work before we lose light." She climbed inside the canoe, still searching. "My dad always tucks them in the back."

"I didn't pack any," Pocahontas said in a small voice.

"What?" Nakoma exclaimed.

"There was no reason we should have needed them," Pocahontas explained. "We were supposed to be back in time."

"Supposed to be," Nakoma said. "But we aren't."

"No," Pocahontas agreed meekly.

The girls stood in silence for several minutes. Pocahontas couldn't tell if the chill she felt was coming from the disappearing sun or the iciness in Nakoma's glare.

"Listen," Pocahontas finally said. "We're

here now and we can't change that. So let's find something to eat, set up a shelter with whatever's around, and build a fire. At least then you can hate me while you're warm and comfortable."

Nakoma let out an exasperated puff of air from her lips. "I'll take care of the shelter. Think you can catch some fish, or was that experience exaggerated, too?"

Pocahontas ignored the jab. "I can catch the fish."

Nakoma marched off into the trees to gather supplies. Pocahontas sighed and set about finding their dinner.

Chapter 6
Getting to Know Each Other

In the last slivers of daylight, Pocahontas brought several small fish up to the makeshift shelter Nakoma had built using the overturned canoe and a few leafy tree branches lashed together with roots.

Nakoma had scoured the nearby trees for dry twigs. She tossed them in the small pit Pocahontas dug for a fire. Pocahontas kneeled down to start it with two small rocks she'd gathered from the river. She struck the rocks against each other, hoping for a spark, but nothing happened. She struck them again, but it was no use. "I've never started a fire this way, but I know it can work," Pocahontas said, looking up at Nakoma's amused face. "I don't think it helps that they're wet."

"Try this." Nakoma pulled a bundle from her satchel and unwrapped a small square-shaped piece of wood.

"You carry that with you?" Pocahontas asked, surprised. The piece of wood had small holes in it. At home, they used a tool like this to start a fire by rubbing a pointy stick in one of the holes to create a spark. Nakoma had even managed to keep it protected and dry in her satchel.

"I like to be prepared," Nakoma said.

Pocahontas gratefully accepted the piece of wood and found a stick nearby. She used the river rock to sharpen the stick, and soon they had a fire going.

The girls sat down next to the blaze. Pocahontas cleaned the fish, and the girls held them over the flames to roast. They watched the fish cook for a while in silence, then Nakoma finally spoke.

"I don't hate you, you know," Nakoma said.

Pocahontas looked at her, eyebrows raised. "You don't?"

"Of course not," Nakoma said. "How could I possibly hate you? You're Pocahontas, daughter of the chief. You're adventurous and brave and strong. You're always doing amazing things, like helping an injured animal, or running faster than all the boys, or chasing a snake away from someone's garden." Nakoma nudged the fish in the fire with a stick, avoiding eye contact. "Or putting yourself in danger to save my little brother."

Pocahontas didn't know what to say. She supposed she had done all those things, but she had no idea Nakoma had been paying attention or even cared. "I put you in danger, too, though," Pocahontas added after a few moments.

"You did," Nakoma agreed. "You're kind of terrible at planning, you know?" Nakoma said this part with a giggle, which made Pocahontas laugh, too.

"I think that's pretty clear," Pocahontas said, motioning to their temporary shelter and broken boat.

"But at the same time," Nakoma continued, "I wish I could be more like you."

"A terrible planner?" Pocahontas asked.

Nakoma shook her head. "Just more . . . free. You go where the wind takes you."

"It must be hard for you to do that when you have your little brother and sister to look after all the time. Every time I see you, you're busy minding them and helping your family with chores. Helping everyone, really." Pocahontas realized as she said this that it was true. Every time she saw her, Nakoma was doing something for someone else.

"Ha," Nakoma sputtered. "Some helper I am. I couldn't even tell my own brother was sick." She bit her lip.

"It's not your fault," Pocahontas said. "When we get back, and Tomoy is healed, and everything is okay again, I promise to help you take care of them."

Nakoma wiped a tear that had just begun to fall. "Why?" she asked, confused.

"Why not?" Pocahontas replied. She removed the fish from the fire and handed one to Nakoma, taking another for herself. "I don't have any little siblings of my own. It would be fun, and you could use the break."

"It's not fun," Nakoma said. "I promise you, it's not fun."

Pocahontas laughed. "We can make it fun," she said.

The girls, overtaken by hunger, ate their dinner without saying anything in between bites. But Pocahontas thought as she chewed. Nakoma was surprising her on this trip. First by being willing to go at all. And second by how easily the girls talked to each other now that they didn't have a river, or bean fields, or younger siblings in between them. Perhaps they could be friends after all.

When their dinner was done and their hungry bellies satisfied, the girls rested next to the fire and looked up at the sky, keeping warm in spite of the increased chill nipping at them.

"I've been thinking," Nakoma said after a few minutes.

"Oh?" Pocahontas asked. She wondered if Nakoma had been thinking about the possibilities of their future friendship, as well.

"Since the boat is broken now and can't go back in the water, I think we should just forget about the plant and walk home when it's light again," Nakoma said.

That was not what Pocahontas had expected to hear. "Are you sure?" she asked.

"I know we'd miss the chance to bring back the medicine for Tomoy, but your father and Kekata believed the men would make it back in time. I'd rather get home so my parents stop worrying." Nakoma's voice was soft through the sound of the crackling fire. Pocahontas knew she wasn't making this decision lightly.

"I think you're right," Pocahontas said.

"You do?" Nakoma sounded surprised.

"I took on more than I could handle," Pocahontas admitted. "We should have listened to the grown-ups. I guess maybe they really do know better."

"Well, not *all* the time." Nakoma giggled.

"No, not all the time," Pocahontas said with a laugh. "Definitely not."

As night fell, the two girls chatted across the fire, learning more about each other, sharing stories about their families, and finding new differences and similarities between them. Although they'd both be in quite a bit of trouble when they returned to their families, home was home, and they couldn't wait to get back there. They soon drifted off into a deep sleep, ready to wake at dawn and face the journey to their village.

Chapter 7
A Thorny Situation

Pocahontas woke as the sun was still rising. When she sat up, she saw that Nakoma was already awake, and apparently had been for some time.

"Good morning!" Nakoma said cheerfully. She handed Pocahontas a heaping pile of berries and chinquapin nuts, served on a big leaf.

"Morning," Pocahontas grumbled. She

was not fond of mornings. It usually took her quite a while to feel the kind of energy Nakoma was showing. "Are these all for me?" Pocahontas asked as she began to pick at the fruit.

"I already had mine," Nakoma said. "The earlier we head out, the earlier we're back."

Pocahontas could tell by the way Nakoma was anxiously hopping around— making sure their fire was out and tidying their campsite—that she would be ready to go the moment Pocahontas was. So Pocahontas finished her breakfast and splashed some river water on her face to help herself wake up.

"All right," Pocahontas said. "Let's go."

The girls first tied a bunch of brightly colored wildflowers to a branch hanging over the river so they'd easily be able to find the canoe later. They'd be in even more trouble if they couldn't help the tribe find and retrieve the damaged boat. Then they set off on foot upriver, navigating through the trees.

"We'll be safest if we just stick close to the riverbank," Pocahontas said. Nakoma agreed.

Within a few yards, however, the trees gave way and the riverbank was completely taken over by thorny wild raspberry bushes. The dense growth was so thick the girls couldn't pass through.

"We'll have to go inland a little, I guess," Pocahontas said. She and Nakoma headed away from the river, looking for a break in the bramble where they could try to crawl through without tearing their clothes and poking their faces with thorns.

But as they walked and walked, the raspberry shrubs continued. There was no end in sight. Then, to their dismay, the ground suddenly sloped upward.

"Oh, no," Nakoma said, following the ground with her eyes. The thorny bushes spread out, up, and over the steep hill. There was no way forward—and no way to continue inland unless they wanted to climb or walk through thorns.

"We could walk a little farther downriver from the campsite," Pocahontas suggested. "Maybe we can find a way to cut inland and go around the bramble there?"

Nakoma scratched her head. "I don't think so. That's the direction I walked to pick the berries for our breakfast. It's pretty much blocked by thorns, too."

"So I guess..." Pocahontas met Nakoma's eyes. They spoke in unison: "We have to get back on the river."

The thought of braving the cold, angry river after what they'd gone through the day before was almost too much to bear. But they didn't have a choice. There was no way out of this section of the forest on foot.

As they walked back to their campsite, Nakoma laid out a plan for repairing the canoe. Pocahontas and Nakoma would gather all the reeds they could find in the clearing. They would weave the reeds into thick mats and cords and use them to plug the cracks and holes in the boat, gluing them into place with tree sap.

It took a couple of hours to find enough reeds to use, but the weaving went quickly — both girls were used to crafting supplies and helping make repairs. When they were sure they'd covered all the damaged parts of the boat, they let it sit in the sun, which was high in the sky. Nakoma said this would help make sure the sap dried.

While they waited, they snacked on more berries and nuts. Pocahontas was glad to have the little food they could find, but her stomach was starting to grumble for more. She thought about the boiled squash and rich, hearty stew she could be eating back at home. Or, even better, a delicious flat corn cake baked fresh in the fire.

"Should we try it out?" Nakoma asked after the girls finished their small lunch.

Pocahontas nodded. She and Nakoma each took a side of the canoe, pushed it into the river, and hopped in. To Pocahontas's great relief, the water felt much calmer than the day before.

The girls let the river carry them downstream, paddling every so often. The canoe's repairs seemed to hold, with no water coming in at their feet.

"It's working!" Nakoma said, delighted.

"Thanks to you!" Pocahontas answered, grinning at her. "You know, now that the boat is all right again, we could just keep going downriver to find the plant."

Nakoma shook her head. "Let's not risk it," she said. "Let's find the fork in the river that loops back home. It's coming up soon, right?"

Pocahontas looked around. While they were repairing the boat, she'd told Nakoma about the river bend that would take them back to their village. It was the way her father always went, and she knew it came just after the rapids—at least, she thought it did. But with the higher water level, everything looked different. And her confidence in her navigation skills was nearly gone after their disaster on the rapids.

"I—" She tried to think of a way to answer Nakoma. "I'm not sure," she finally said. "It should be, but . . ."

"But what?" Nakoma asked.

"But I can't say for sure," Pocahontas finally admitted. She didn't want to tell Nakoma something she wasn't certain about.

"Ugh," Nakoma said. "I can't believe this. Are you sure of *anything*?"

Pocahontas searched for the words to answer.

"Did you really even see the plant when you were on that fishing trip with your father? Or were you just looking for an excuse to go on a fun little adventure?"

"I saw it!" Pocahontas defended herself. She *had* seen it. She was sure of that much. Wasn't she? The sudden fear that maybe she had been wrong all along crept in. She'd made so many mistakes already.

"Nothing good has come from this trip," Nakoma continued. "We're just lost."

Pocahontas continued rowing, staring at the river water bubbling around the paddle. She felt like the paddle right now. Trying to move in one direction while all the force of the water pushed against it in the other.

She closed her eyes. Her father always tried to teach her not to react with anger. To think about words before she said them. Words spoken became a part of the water, the earth, the air; they flowed back into the water her people drank, nourished the seeds they planted, and filled the air they breathed.

"The river was calling to me," Pocahontas said finally. "It was. Maybe you think that's because I'm silly, or because I wanted to get into mischief. And maybe you're right. But I really did think we had a chance to help Tomoy." She gulped.

She went on. "And yesterday I thought that even if every other part of this outing was a failure, maybe the reason the river was calling to me was so that we could go on this adventure together and become friends." Pocahontas stared ahead at the water, without facing Nakoma. "But maybe I was wrong about that, too."

Nakoma was silent. The only sounds were the swoosh of the river and birds chirping and flitting through the trees. "Pocahontas—" she finally began.

"Oh!" Pocahontas shouted suddenly, interrupting her. "Look!"

A swift movement on the riverbank up ahead had caught Pocahontas's attention. As Nakoma started to speak, Pocahontas realized it was a small animal—and he was in trouble!

"Paddle over!" Nakoma called to Pocahontas. The girls began to paddle

toward the animal, their argument temporarily forgotten. As they got closer, Pocahontas saw that it was a baby raccoon. He was stuck on a branch poking out over the riverbank, scrabbling desperately to pull himself up onto land. But the river current, despite being calmer that day, was lapping at the branch, and the small creature was no match for its strength. The raccoon was dangerously close to falling in and being swept away.

Once their canoe was near enough, Pocahontas reached her paddle out toward the raccoon. As soon as the raccoon noticed the sturdier stick, he grabbed it and clung with all four paws. Pocahontas hoisted the paddle up and over the riverbank so the animal could reach safety. The raccoon stretched one paw out to test the ground. Seeming satisfied with its solid surface, he let go of the paddle and crawled onto the dirt. He curled up in a ball, breathing hard, his fur wet.

"He must be exhausted," Nakoma said.

The boat was close enough to the shore that Pocahontas could touch the riverbank. "I'm just going to make sure he's okay," she said. Nakoma nodded.

Pocahontas climbed out of the boat and onto shore. As soon as she leaned over the raccoon, though, his eyes bolted open and he ran off, away from the shoreline.

"Wait!" Pocahontas shouted, and she took off after the raccoon. If he was in shock or injured, he would make an easy target for a larger animal.

The little gray bundle of fur scampered through the forest, almost too fast for Pocahontas to keep up. He whipped around trees, hopped over roots, and clambered through bushes. Just when she thought she'd lost sight of him, Pocahontas rounded a large tree trunk and saw that the raccoon had stopped in front of a thicket of raspberry bushes. He pulled berries off a bush with his front paws, shoving them in his cheeks as fast as he could pick them.

"So that's where you were running off to!" Pocahontas laughed as she walked toward the raccoon. Then she stopped. *This place is familiar,* she thought. She whirled around, taking in every inch of the land. She walked past the raccoon, a bit farther along the raspberry thicket.

And there, just as she'd remembered, was the cluster of white flowering plants that would save Tomoy.

Chapter 8
The Plant

"Nakoma!" Pocahontas ran back to the river as fast as her feet would take her. When she reached the boat, she choked out between breaths, "The plant! I thought the spot was much farther downriver, but I was wrong! It's here!"

Nakoma jumped out of the canoe, and the two girls quickly but carefully pulled it ashore. Then Pocahontas led her to the raspberry grove, where the raccoon was still stuffing his face with berries, his cheek fur stained with red juice.

"That's it?" Nakoma asked Pocahontas, approaching the delicate white-and-green plants.

"That's it," Pocahontas said. Nakoma opened the satchel she'd brought from home in anticipation of this moment. The girls set to work gathering as much of the medicinal plant as they could carry. After several minutes of quietly harvesting together, Nakoma spoke.

"Thank you," she said.

"For this?" Pocahontas asked. "You don't need to thank me."

"I do," Nakoma said. "Thank you for wanting to help."

"Even if my helping got us stuck on the river with a broken boat?"

"It's not broken anymore," Nakoma said, grinning.

Pocahontas laughed. "True. But maybe wait to thank me until we've made it *back* with the medicine."

"Deal," Nakoma said.

Once Nakoma's satchel was full of the plants, much more than Tomoy needed and hopefully more than anyone in their village ever would, they were ready to head back out on the river.

"Let's take some berries for the trip," Pocahontas said. She was learning from Nakoma that it was a good idea to be prepared; even if she wasn't hungry yet, she would be later. She began plucking berries from the part of the bush that was too high for the raccoon. The raccoon, his belly plump and full, was sprawled out on the ground, a look of bliss on his face.

When they had finished picking berries, Nakoma and Pocahontas began to walk back to their boat. Pocahontas heard a rustling sound behind them as they walked. She turned around to see the raccoon following them. "Go on," Pocahontas called back to the creature. "Find your family. You're safe now."

But the raccoon didn't listen, and he continued to follow them all the way back to the canoe. Nakoma and Pocahontas each gripped the edge of the boat, preparing to hoist it back into the water. Before they lifted it, though, the raccoon clawed his way up the side of the boat and climbed inside.

"Excuse me," Nakoma said, giggling.

Pocahontas lifted the creature up and set him back down on the riverbank. "You don't want to go where we're going." The raccoon, ignoring Pocahontas, crawled right back in the boat. She lifted him up again. "No, really," she said, this time looking the animal in the eyes. "You nearly drowned out there. The river is no place for a raccoon. Stay here, where it's safe."

The raccoon stared back at Pocahontas. He looked at her so intently, she wondered if he was actually understanding her words. Then, suddenly, he reached a paw into her bag, grabbed a handful of berries, shoved them in his mouth, and crawled back into the boat.

"I think he wants to come," Nakoma said, shrugging.

Pocahontas sighed. "We're not rescuing you again," she told the raccoon, wagging her finger at him. She knew, of course, that she would rescue him again in a heartbeat.

The girls lifted the boat into the water and jumped in. They paddled back out to the center of the river. The raccoon ran along the inside of the boat toward the front. "Wait!" Pocahontas shouted, nervous. But the raccoon just perched at the bow so he could get a better look at the journey ahead. "You're a very strange animal," she said, shaking her head. It was as though he had not recently been in danger on that very same river.

As the canoe drifted, Nakoma asked, "Which way now? The river bend has to be close, right? Or should we turn around and head upriver?"

Pocahontas chewed her lip. The loop in the river would be the safest way home, but she hated the thought of drifting farther and farther away from home to find it. Before she answered, though, Nakoma splashed a paddle in the water, crying, "Wait!"

What now? Pocahontas thought. The

raccoon was chittering in an excited way and pointing at a bend in the river just ahead. Nakoma was squinting in the same direction.

"I know this place," Nakoma said.

"You do?" Pocahontas asked. It wasn't the river bend she'd been looking for, the route her father usually took.

Nakoma pointed her paddle toward the river bend. "Paddle in that direction," she said confidently.

Pocahontas followed Nakoma's instructions. The baby raccoon gripped the front of the boat, letting his fur catch the spray from the paddles as they dipped in and out of the river. He didn't seem to mind the water in the slightest.

As the canoe headed toward the bend, Pocahontas saw that the river branched off there into a narrow stream. Nakoma and Pocahontas guided the canoe through. The intense sunlight began to fade, shielded from view by lush, thick tree canopies overhead. The stream was calm, a gentle, quiet cousin to the louder, harsher river they'd just left behind.

"Where are we?" Pocahontas whispered to Nakoma. She didn't know why her voice had come out in a whisper; it just seemed like the right tone for the serene air that surrounded them.

"This is where Grandmother Willow lives," Nakoma answered.

Pocahontas was confused. "Your . . . your grandmother? But I just saw your grandmother back in the village. She doesn't—"

"Not *my* grandmother, Pocahontas," Nakoma said. "Grandmother Willow is everyone's grandmother."

Pocahontas still didn't understand. "What do you mean?" she asked.

"Look!" Nakoma pointed.

Up ahead, the stream opened into a large lagoon. In the heart of the lagoon rose a massive, ancient willow tree. The leafy

branches stretched all the way down to the water. The girls paddled toward the tree and through the curtain of leaves.

It was as though they were entering a secret hideaway.

The raccoon leapt from the canoe and onto a root bulging from the water. "Hey!" Pocahontas shouted, but the raccoon didn't stop. He scampered along the root toward the tree and then climbed straight up the trunk. As his paws hit the bark, the tree began to shift and move. Pocahontas blinked, unsure if she could believe what she was seeing. But it was clear—in the trunk of the tree, a kind, almost human face had appeared.

Chapter 9
Grandmother Willow

"**C**ome on," Nakoma urged, her voice soft. Pocahontas hadn't realized they'd both stopped paddling once the raccoon jumped out of the boat. They slowly steered the canoe closer to the tree.

"Is *that* Grandmother Willow?" Pocahontas asked Nakoma.

"Yes," Nakoma answered. "I haven't been here since I was Alawa's age, but I could never forget her."

Pocahontas understood why. As the boat drifted toward the base of the tree, Grandmother Willow's face looming directly overhead, Pocahontas suddenly felt shy.

Grandmother Willow's cheeks twitched with laughter as the raccoon crawled across what looked like her eyebrows to rest on a branch sprouting from the side of her trunk. "You've had quite an adventure," the tree said, shifting her eyes down to the girls in the canoe.

Pocahontas gulped, so in awe of this incredible being in front of her that she didn't know what to say.

"Grandmother Willow," Nakoma began,

"I'm Nakoma. I met you when I was—"

"You were here five years ago," Grandmother Willow interrupted. "A shame you haven't been back since. I would have loved to see more of you. I haven't been getting nearly as many visitors as I used to."

"You remember me?" Nakoma asked, surprised.

"Of course I do." Grandmother Willow chuckled. "I remember everything." She turned her eyes to Pocahontas. "Including your mother, Pocahontas."

Pocahontas nearly dropped her paddle in surprise. "My mother?" she exclaimed, her shyness forgotten.

"Mm-hmm," the old tree murmured. "She never let a season go by without taking a canoe down here to pay me a visit. Always finding one excuse or another to get out on the river." Grandmother Willow winked. "Sound familiar?"

Pocahontas was still in shock. "But how do you know who I am?"

Grandmother Willow grinned. "I knew you before you were born, my dear. Why, I never saw more of your mother than when she was expecting your arrival. We talked about you all the time . . . what you would be like, what you would do together, what she would teach you." Her branches bristled, almost shivering. "You look just like her."

Pocahontas blinked away a tear, stunned into silence. That was her mother's special place. Those waters. That soil. That forest. Her mother had been there. Pocahontas had never felt so grateful for anything; she had never felt so close to the mother she'd barely known and couldn't remember at all.

Nakoma cleared her throat. "Grandmother Willow, we need your help to get home," she said.

"Oh, I'll bet you do." Grandmother Willow laughed. "With the weather lately, it's quite a miracle you're here at all. I'd guess that you didn't have permission to take that canoe?"

Pocahontas and Nakoma both blushed.

"And seeing those fresh patches—nice handiwork, by the way—I'm going to guess you now understand why you didn't have permission?" Grandmother Willow asked.

The girls nodded.

"Then I'll spare you my lecturing. Tell me all about it."

The story tumbled out of Nakoma and Pocahontas, the girls taking turns to recount their experiences over the past couple of days.

Grandmother Willow listened patiently,

without interruption. The raccoon, on the other hand, got very excited when the girls reached the part about rescuing him from the river. He paced back and forth along the tree branch, then rubbed his belly longingly as they talked about the berries.

"And then we found you," Nakoma finished.

"That you did," Grandmother Willow said. "Sounds like you found more than this old lagoon. You found adventure, you found danger, you found medicine, you found Meeko—"

"Meeko?" Pocahontas asked. "What's a Meeko?"

The raccoon ran down the side of the tree trunk and leapt back into the boat. He scrambled up to Pocahontas, patted her on the cheek, and then settled right down into her lap. "I see," Pocahontas said, realizing Grandmother Willow was talking about the raccoon. "Meeko."

"How do you know his name?" Nakoma asked.

"I gave him that name," Grandmother Willow said. "I practically raised this little scamp. He showed up here all alone one day, no family in sight. Even smaller than he is now, if you can imagine. But," the tree sighed, "I've barely been able to help him find enough food. The amount that animal can *eat!*"

Nakoma and Pocahontas giggled. They had become well aware of the raccoon's appetite in the short time they'd known him.

"It was smart of him to find some humans to cozy up to," Grandmother Willow said. "Just keep an eye on the food stores when you get back home."

"He didn't find us," Pocahontas said. "We found him, remember?"

"Of course," Grandmother Willow said, raising an eyebrow at Meeko. "That's what he'd like you to think. He's a clever one."

Pocahontas eyed the raccoon snuggled in her lap. He almost looked like he was grinning.

"So, can you help us find our way back home, Grandmother Willow?" Nakoma asked.

"Ah, yes." Grandmother Willow blinked. "I was interrupted before. As I was saying . . . you found more than you were looking for on this journey of yours. You also found courage, you found your own strength, and you found friendship."

Pocahontas and Nakoma looked at each other. The girls smiled. They had been through a lot. Nothing would ever change that. Nakoma laughed nervously. "I wish that could help us get home, though."

"Why, of course it will," Grandmother Willow said. "With those tools on your side? You girls can do anything—especially if you're together."

Nakoma and Pocahontas beamed with pride.

"But next time, do it with your parents' permission. All right?" Grandmother Willow frowned at them.

"All right," Pocahontas and Nakoma answered in unison.

"Now, on the other side of the lagoon, there's an outlet to another part of the river. . . ." Grandmother Willow gave the girls instructions for how to take the loop of the river back home—a route that *wouldn't* take them back across the rapids. She even tested the wind with her leaves, assuring the girls that they'd have a smooth journey back to the village.

With replenished spirits and full hearts,

Pocahontas and Nakoma bid goodbye to Grandmother Willow, promising to visit her again soon. Meeko ran out of the canoe to give the tree a hug, his tiny paws covering barely a fraction of the massive trunk. Then he darted back to the boat, resuming his position on the bow for the journey home.

Chapter 10
Home Again

The ride back to the village was smooth and uneventful, thanks to Grandmother Willow's instructions. Pocahontas couldn't help wishing the trip downriver had gone as well.

But then she remembered Grandmother Willow's words about how much more she and Nakoma had found on their trip besides the medicine. If it hadn't been for all the trouble the girls had gotten into, and if they'd found the plant as quickly and easily as Pocahontas had planned, would she and Nakoma even be friends? Would they have found Meeko? Would Pocahontas have ever met Grandmother Willow and heard about her mother?

In the end, she believed, everything had happened the way it was supposed to. She just hoped that Nakoma's brother had kept his strength up while they were away.

The scouts spotted Pocahontas and Nakoma before they even reached the shore. Men and women from the village rushed out to meet their boat and help them onto land. There was barely a word exchanged once they saw what the girls had brought back. The girls ran to Kekata's lodge, where Pocahontas's father was standing outside. His stern face broke into relief when he saw the girls approaching. He kneeled down and scooped them into a giant hug.

"My brother?" Nakoma asked.

"He's inside," Chief Powhatan said, gesturing toward the door. Nakoma darted in with her satchel full of the plant.

"Please," Pocahontas said, looking into her father's eyes. "Can I see him, too?" Chief Powhatan sighed.

"Go," he said to his daughter.

Pocahontas shoved Meeko into her father's arms. The raccoon sniffed the chief's face curiously. "He's probably hungry," she said, and she ran inside to join Nakoma.

Inside, Kekata was already stripping the plant, crushing up its roots, and steeping them in hot water to make a tea. Nakoma's mother was holding Nakoma tightly. Tomoy lay on a mat, a wet cloth on his forehead, his eyes fluttering and his cheeks burning.

The healer spooned the tea into the boy's mouth, one sip at a time, until it was gone. Tomoy murmured and cried softly, his breathing heavy. But soon the red in his cheeks began to ease. He moaned softly and sighed in relief.

"He'll be cured?" Nakoma asked Kekata.

The healer brushed the boy's damp hair away from his forehead. He nodded.

Nakoma and her parents wept for joy. They gathered Pocahontas into their hug, and they all cried tears of happiness together.

* * *

In the following days, everything slowly went back to normal. The men returned home with more of the healing plants, and the medicine was prepared and stored. Tomoy recovered from his fever and became healthy enough to walk, play, and even bother his older sister. And after discovering the gardens, Meeko was, for a moment, finally full.

Nakoma and Pocahontas were celebrated and applauded for their bravery and for saving Tomoy. But Pocahontas's father was never one to let an opportunity for learning from mistakes slip by. The chief had observed

how well Nakoma and Pocahontas had worked together on their river adventure, and how well they'd repaired the canoe after it took a beating on the rapids. So for their punishment, Chief Powhatan ordered the girls to use their new skills to repair the rest of the village's boats—even the giant ones that could hold up to forty men!

"It could be worse," Pocahontas said as she helped Nakoma apply a coat of sap to their fifth canoe. She couldn't remember a time when her fingers hadn't been sticky.

"Oh, really?" Nakoma asked.

"We could be weaving baskets or something," Pocahontas said.

"But I like weaving baskets!" Nakoma cried.

"Of course you do," Pocahontas said. The girls giggled. They sifted through their mound of supplies to select another reed. Before they could find it, Meeko crashed through the pile, his paws kicking bowls and reeds and bark everywhere.

"Meeko!" Nakoma and Pocahontas yelled. But Meeko didn't seem to hear them. He kept running, a hummingbird hot on his tail.

"That raccoon"—Pocahontas shook her

head—"always making the strangest friends."

"Speaking of which," Nakoma said, beginning to pick up the supplies Meeko had knocked over, "what do you say about a trip to see Grandmother Willow?"

"Really?" Pocahontas exclaimed. "You're ready to sneak out again so soon?"

"I didn't say anything about sneaking." Nakoma laughed. "This would be a *planned* trip. Organized in advance. With supplies. And permission."

"Oh," Pocahontas said. "I guess I'm okay with that."

"Great!" Nakoma said. "You'll talk to your dad, and I'll talk to my parents. We'll choose a day, and we can leave at sunrise if the weather is good. We'll need satchels, some dried meat and rockahominy, and let's *not* forget mats for shelter this time—"

"Nakoma," Pocahontas interrupted.

"Yeah?"

Pocahontas splashed her friend in the face with river water. Nakoma screamed in surprise, blinking the water out of her eyes. She looked for a moment like she was going to yell at Pocahontas. But instead she burst out laughing, then splashed Pocahontas back. They kept splashing, playing in the water, forgetting about the repairs.

At that rate, Pocahontas knew their

punishment was going to last several weeks longer than it was supposed to. But she didn't mind. With Nakoma, it was as much about the journey as it was about the destination. Now that she'd found a friend, everything they did together could be an adventure.

Disney Before the Story

Mulan's
Secret Plan

By TESSA ROEHL   ILLUSTRATED BY DENISE...

Disney Before the Story

Elsa's
Icy Rescue

...EGAN   ILLUSTRATED BY MARIO CORTES

Read all the Before the Story books!

Disney Before the Story

Anna
Finds a Friend

By KATE EGAN   ILLUSTRATED BY ELIZABETTA MELARANCI

Cinderella
Takes the Stage

By TESSA ROEHL   ILLUSTRATED BY ADRIENNE BROWN